FIVE Little MONKEYS
reading in bed

For information about permission to reproduce
selections from this book, write to Permissions,
Houghton Mifflin Harcourt Publishing Company,
215 Park Avenue South, New York, New York 10003.

www.hmhco.com

Library of Congress Cataloging-in-Publication Data
Christelow, Eileen.
Five little monkeys reading in bed /
by Eileen Christelow.
p. cm.
Summary: Mama has said it is time for "Lights out!
Sweet dreams! No more reading in bed," but her
five little monkeys cannot resist reading just a few
more books to one another.
[1. Stories in rhyme. 2. Books and reading—Fiction.
3. Bedtime—Fiction. 4. Monkeys—Fiction.
5. Mother and child—Fiction. 6. Behavior—Fiction.]
I. Title.
PZ8.3.C456Fjm 2011
[E]—dc22
2010043397

ISBN: 978-0-547-38610-2 hardcover
ISBN: 978-0-544-48800-7 paperback

Manufactured in China
SCP 10 9 8 7 6 5 4 3 2
4500573662

For the latest batch of monkeys:
Hazel, Leo, and Nola May

FIVE Little MONKEYS
reading in bed

Eileen Christelow

HOUGHTON MIFFLIN HARCOURT

Boston   New York

WHEN the five little monkeys are ready for bed,
their Mama reads stories, then kisses each head.

"It's bedtime for monkeys! Now turn out the light."
"Oh, Mama! Oh, PLEASE! One more story tonight!"

But Mama's too tired. She's read more than four.
"Lights out! Sweet dreams!" She closes their door.

One monkey whispers, "This book looks so good!
If Mama won't read it, then maybe we could."

Then out come the tissues. They ALL start to bawl.
They sob and they cry till the last page of all.

What happens next?

Oh, no!

"I think I'm lost," said the puppy.

It's such a good ending, their sobs turn to cheers.
Those monkeys are LOUD! (You should cover your ears!)

In fact, they're so noisy that Mama runs in.
"What's all this racket? This chaos? This din?"

One monkey admits with a guilt-ridden look,
"We've been reading the very best, happy, sad book!"

Mama raises an eyebrow. "What was it I said?"

Then one monkey sighs as she turns out the light.
"I wish we could read this new ghost book tonight."

One monkey starts hooting—an eerie ghost sound.
And soon they're all wailing and jumping around!

Then a dark, spooky shadow appears on the wall.
But a knock on their door is what frightens them ALL!

. . . Mama walks in!
"What's all this racket?
This chaos? This din?"

The monkeys all gasp. "We thought YOU were the ghost!
This book is so scary. We like it the most!"
Mama raises an eyebrow. "What was it I said?"

19

One monkey shivers. "That book was so creepy, so GOOD but so scary, I'll never be sleepy!"

She pulls out a joke book. "We've got to be quiet."
But the jokes are so funny! In fact, they're a riot!

The monkeys try hard not to giggle or laugh.
But then there's a joke with a foolish giraffe.

It's so silly, so goofy, they all start to roar!
And then can you guess who flings open their door?

Oh, yes! It's Mama! She comes storming right in.
"What's all this racket? This chaos? This din?"

The monkeys keep giggling. They JUST cannot quit!
Mama picks up their books. "I've had it! That's it!"
Then she raises an eyebrow. "Did you hear what I said?"

Lights out! Sweet dreams!
No more reading in bed!

Well, the monkeys are tired. They're almost asleep
when they hear someone giggle, then laugh, and then weep.

"Do you hear all that noise? And just WHO can it BE?"
"Let's sneak down the hall." (Can you guess what they see?)

"Oh, Mama!" they giggle. "What was it you said?"

31

32

Those monkeys are sleepy! They head out the door.
"Just wait till tomorrow, and then we'll read more!"